BORROWER'S CARD   1023

The Dancers

Walter Dean Myers   SCHOOL LIBRARY

1023

THE DANCERS

by Walter Dean Myers

pictures by Anne Rockwell

Parents' Magazine Press / New York

To my parents, Herbert and Florence Dean,
whose love makes all things possible

"Would you like to come to work with me today, Michael?" Michael's father had put on his jacket and was picking up his tool box.

"Can I help you on your job?" Michael asked.

"No, I'm afraid not. But you can come to the theater and watch me. And if you promise to be very quiet, you can watch the dancers practice, too."

So Michael went on the subway

with his father to the theater.

It was Saturday morning and the theater was empty —just rows and rows of dark, empty seats. His father led him to a seat in the first row.

"Now sit very still," he said, "and watch."

On the stage there were people working. Some of them were moving lights around. They were the biggest lights Michael had ever seen.

Then his father and some other men began bringing trees onto the stage. The trees were made of cloth and wire, but Michael thought they looked very real. There were short trees and tall trees and even a few large rocks. It was like watching a whole forest grow in a few minutes.

After a while some musicians came in and started playing. They didn't seem to be playing anything in particular, just making noises. Michael's father came down and sat next to him.

"What are they playing?" Michael asked.

"They aren't playing anything, yet," his father said. "They're just warming up."

Then some dancers came onto the stage. They began twisting and stretching and jumping about. Then they stopped and Michael's father whispered, "Now we have to be very quiet. They're ready to dance."

A tall man lifted his arms, and when he brought them
down all the musicians began to play. On the stage the
dancers were very still, almost like dolls. Then one of
them moved, just a little. First her arm moved and her
fingers spread across her face, and suddenly she was
dancing.

She looked like a bird flying slowly across the stage. Michael thought that at any moment she might fly away over all their heads. Now another dancer was moving—and another—and another, until they were all dancing. They were like a flock of birds, waving their arms or gently gliding as they turned.

After a minute had passed, the music suddenly changed and another dancer leaped onto the stage. He was bigger than the others, and Michael thought he looked like a very ferocious bird as he moved quickly about.

The ferocious bird began chasing the others, and they all flew off the stage except for the bird who had first started to fly. She tried to get away, but wherever she went the ferocious bird followed her.

Michael could hardly sit in his chair. In front of him the musicians were playing very fast. One of them, playing a violin, was standing as the others sat.

The ferocious bird chased the other one around and around and around until he finally caught her. Then the music changed again. It was slow now, and very sad. The lovely bird lifted her arms once more, slowly, and then fell to the ground.

The music stopped. The dancers didn't move, and for a moment it was very quiet. Then Michael stood up and clapped his hands as loudly as he could because he thought the dancing had been so good.

The dancers and the musicians all looked at Michael. The dancer who had fallen got up. She came down from the stage and came over to Michael.

"Thank you," she said, holding out her hand. "I am Yvonne. And who are you?"

"Michael."

"Do you come to the ballet often, Michael?"

"No, this is my first time. I came with my father."

"Oh, I see. Did you like it?"

"Yes, but I'm sorry he caught you."

Yvonne smiled. "Well, just like some stories and plays, some ballets have sad endings, too. You should see the entire ballet, Michael. I can get tickets for you, and I'd like you to see me dance again."

"Thank you," Michael said. "And I'd like for you to come see me at my house, too. Daddy, can she come to our house?"

"I don't think so, Michael," Yvonne said. "I'm so very busy right now. I'm really sorry."

"I'm sorry, too," Michael said.

"All of the dancers are very busy, Michael," his father told him. "They have to dance and practice and travel to different theaters."

"Good-bye, Michael," Yvonne said, "and thank you for asking me to come to your house."

Michael said good-bye to the dancers and then he went home with his father.

One afternoon a few days later, Michael's mother was cooking dinner and Michael was playing Giant Steps on the sidewalk with Karen and Darlene and Jimmy. They saw a long shiny car pulling up to the curb, right in front of Michael's house.

They stopped playing and watched as three people got out. Suddenly Michael cried, "Look! It's Yvonne!" Then Michael recognized one of the men with her. He was the dancer who had chased Yvonne on the stage, but he didn't look at all like a ferocious bird now.

"Hello, Michael," Yvonne said. "I've come to see you."

"Hello," he answered. "But how did you know where I lived?"

"The people at the theater told me where your father lived so I knew that I would find you here, too."

"I thought you would be too busy."

"I am. I told my manager I was too busy to rehearse today because I was going to see an old friend. How's that?"

"That's just fine!" Michael said, and he grinned.

"Are you really a dancer?" asked Karen who lived next door to Michael.

"Yes, I am," Yvonne replied.

"Can you do the Chicken?" Karen asked.

"The what?"

"She doesn't dance like that, silly," Michael said.
"She hops around and spins and jumps and wiggles her
feet. Like this." Michael raised his hands above his head
as high as he could and then spun around and jumped
and tried to wiggle his feet. But he fell instead.

All the children giggled, and Karen said, "That sure must be a funny dance."

"It's really nice when *she* does it," Michael said.

"Can you do it now?" Karen asked.

"Maybe just a little." Yvonne nodded to one of the men who went to the car and brought back a violin. She and the other dancer both changed their shoes while the man with the violin got ready to play.

Then he began to play very softly and the dancers began to dance.

"Oh, *ballet!* I *love* ballet dancing," Karen exclaimed.
They spun around and around. Across the potsie
squares, around the fire hydrant and over the drawing
that Darlene had made on the sidewalk.

The barber came out of his shop and watched. The television repairman came out, and the old man who was the super in Michael's building sat on the top step of the stoop so he could see better.

"Dance, Michael!" Yvonne called out as she spun around. "Dance!"

Michael put one foot out, just a little—just a little—and then brought it back.

"Dance, everybody, dance!" Yvonne called.

Karen put her arms out and spun slowly to the music, and then Darlene did and Jimmy and finally Michael. Everyone was dancing.

Up and down the stoop and around the fire hydrant

and over the potsie squares they danced.
And danced. And danced.

When the violin finally stopped and the dance was over, all of the children clapped for the dancers and for themselves. Then Michael's mother came out and invited Yvonne and her friends upstairs for dinner. Karen came, too.

Michael's house was full of collard green smells and cornbread smells and fried chicken smells. His mother and his father were smiling when they came in. The table was set with the best plates, the ones with the blue birds on them.

It was a good dinner and everyone enjoyed it, Michael and Karen and the dancers and the violin player.

After dinner Yvonne asked Karen if she would teach her the dance that she knew. So they put on a record and Michael and Karen did the Chicken.

Yvonne watched how Karen did it. Then she did the
Chicken with Michael. Yvonne couldn't do the Chicken
as well as Karen, though.

The violin player laughed and the other dancer
laughed.

But Yvonne hugged Karen and Michael and thanked them both for teaching her a new dance. Then she said that she had had a wonderful time but it was time to go. Everybody said good-bye, and Yvonne invited them all to the ballet.

Finally the night came when they went to the ballet. This time all the seats were filled with people, and the lights on the stage were very bright. Michael saw the violin player sitting with the other musicians.

Michael and Karen tried to sit still, but every once in a while their arms would move with the music and their feet would wiggle under the seats. And they could almost feel that they were dancing, too.

Walter Dean Myers is the author of *Where Does the Day Go?* published by Parents' Magazine Press and awarded first prize for picture books by the Council on Interracial Books for Children in 1969. Born in West Virginia, Mr. Myers now lives in New York City and is employed as a senior editor in publishing. He attended the college of the City of New York where he contributed poetry and fiction to the CCNY literary magazine. His work has also been published in *The Liberator, Black World* (formerly *Negro Digest*) and *The Delta Review*. Another of his picture books soon to be published is titled *The Dragon Takes a Wife*.

Anne Rockwell's first book, *Paul and Arthur Search for the Egg*, was cited as one of the fifty best books of the year by the American Institute of Graphic Arts, and since then she has both written and illustrated many beautiful books for young readers including *Gypsy Girl's Best Shoes, When the Drum Sang, The Monkey's Whiskers* and *Tuhurahura and the Whale*, all published by Parents' Magazine Press. Also for our list she has illustrated *Mexicali Soup, The Glass Valentine, The Three Visitors* and *Eric and the Little Canal Boat*. Mrs. Rockwell lives in Old Greenwich, Connecticut, with her husband, artist Harlow Rockwell, and their three children.